W9-CTT-971

Franklin and the Tin Flute

From an episode of the animated TV series *Franklin*,
produced by Nelvana Limited, Neurones France s.a.r.l. and
Neurones Luxembourg S.A, based on the Franklin books
by Paulette Bourgeois and Brenda Clark.

Story written by Sharon Jennings.

Illustrated by Céleste Gagnon, Sasha McIntyre, Robert Penman and Laura Vegys.

Based on the TV episode *Franklin's Family Treasure*, written by Patrick Granleese.

Kids Can Read is a trademark of Kids Can Press Ltd.

Franklin

Franklin is a trademark of Kids Can Press Ltd.
The character of Franklin was created by Paulette Bourgeois and Brenda Clark.
Text © 2005 Contextx Inc.
Illustrations © 2005 Brenda Clark Illustrator Inc.

All rights reserved. No part of this publication may be reproduced, stored in a
retrieval system or transmitted, in any form or by any means, without the prior
written permission of Kids Can Press Ltd. or, in case of photocopying or other
reprographic copying, a license from The Canadian Copyright Licensing Agency
(Access Copyright). For an Access Copyright license, visit www.accesscopyright.ca or
call toll free to 1-800-893-5777.

Kids Can Press acknowledges the financial support of the Government of Ontario,
through the Ontario Media Development Corporation's Ontario Book Initiative; the
Ontario Arts Council; the Canada Council for the Arts; and the Government of
Canada, through the BPIDP, for our publishing activity.

Published in Canada by
Kids Can Press Ltd.
29 Birch Avenue
Toronto, ON M4V 1E2

Published in the U.S. by
Kids Can Press Ltd.
2250 Military Road
Tonawanda, NY 14150

www.kidscanpress.com

Series editor: Tara Walker
Edited by Yvette Ghione
Designed by Céleste Gagnon

Printed and bound in China

The hardcover edition of this book is smyth sewn casebound.
The paperback edition of this book is limp sewn with a drawn-on cover.

CM 05 0 9 8 7 6 5 4 3 2 1
CM PA 05 0 9 8 7 6 5 4 3 2 1

Library and Archives Canada Cataloguing in Publication

Jennings, Sharon
     Franklin and the tin flute / Sharon Jennings ; illustrated by
Céleste Gagnon ... [et al.].

(Kids Can read)
The character Franklin was created by Paulette Bourgeois and
Brenda Clark.

ISBN 1-55337-800-8 (bound). ISBN 1-55337-801-6 (pbk.)

I. Gagnon, Céleste II. Bourgeois, Paulette III. Clark, Brenda IV. Title. V. Series: Kids
Can read (Toronto, Ont.)

PS8569.E563F7175 2005   jC813'.54   C2004-904712-4

Kids Can Press is a  Entertainment company

Franklin and the Tin Flute

Kids Can Press

MINITONAS EARLY YEARS SCHOOL

Franklin can tie his shoes.

Franklin can count by twos.

And Franklin can play the triangle
and the tambourine.

But Franklin cannot play a tin flute.

So when Franklin found a tin flute,
he gave it away.

Now, Franklin needs it back.

One day, Franklin was playing

in the basement.

He found an old box.

Inside was a tin flute.

Franklin picked it up and blew.

Twack!

"Ugh," said Franklin.

He blew the flute again.

Toot! Tweak!

"Hmmm,"

said Franklin.

"Maybe I will get

better with practice."

Franklin played the flute
all morning.

Toot! Toot! Tweak! Tweak!

"Hmmm," said Franklin.

"I am not getting better.

I am getting *worse!*"

Franklin went to the park.

On the way, he blew the tin flute

again and again.

Twack! Toot! Tweak!

Tweak! Toot! Twack!

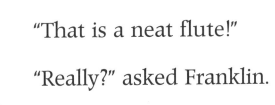

"Wow!" said Rabbit.

"That is a neat flute!"

"Really?" asked Franklin.

"I'll trade you for it,"

said Rabbit.

He held out his best,

green marble.

"It's a deal!"

said Franklin.

At lunchtime, Franklin showed everyone his marble.

"I got it from Rabbit," he said.

"I saw Rabbit on my way home," said Franklin's father.

"He was playing a tin flute."

"I know," said Franklin. "I gave —"

"It was just like *my* old tin flute," said Franklin's father.

"It belonged to your grandpa."

"Uh-oh," said Franklin.

"I am going to go look for it,"
said Franklin's father.

"I am going to go look for Rabbit,"
said Franklin.

Franklin found Rabbit in the sandbox.

He gave him his marble.

"I need my tin flute back,"

said Franklin.

"It was my grandpa's."

"Sorry, Franklin,"
said Rabbit.
"I traded it to Bear
for his pail
and shovel."

"Oh, no!"
cried Franklin.
"I have to find Bear!"

Franklin and Rabbit found Bear

at the pond.

Rabbit gave Bear his pail and shovel.

"I need my tin flute back,"

said Franklin.

"It was his grandpa's," said Rabbit.

"Sorry, Franklin," said Bear.

"I traded it to Goose for her sailboat."

"Oh, no!" cried Franklin.

"I have to find Goose!"

Franklin and Rabbit and Bear

found Goose in the library.

Bear gave Goose her sailboat.

"I need my

tin flute back,"

said Franklin.

"It was his grandpa's,"

said Bear.

"Sorry, Franklin,"

said Goose.

"I traded it to Fox

for his crayons."

"Oh, no!"

cried Franklin.

"I have to find Fox!"

MINITONAS EARLY YEARS SCHOOL

Franklin and Rabbit and Bear

and Goose found Fox on the hill.

Goose gave Fox his crayons.

"I need my tin flute back,"

said Franklin.

"It was his grandpa's," said Goose.

"Sorry, Franklin," said Fox.

"I traded it to Skunk for her kite."

"Oh, no!" cried Franklin.

"I have to find Skunk!"

Franklin and Rabbit and Bear

and Goose and Fox found Skunk

at home.

Fox gave Skunk her kite.

"I need my tin flute back,"

said Franklin.

"It was his grandpa's,"

said Fox.

"Sorry, Franklin,"
said Skunk.
"I traded it to Beaver
for her book."

"Oh, no!" cried Franklin.
"I have to find Beaver!"

23

Franklin and Rabbit and Bear

and Goose and Fox and Skunk

looked everywhere for Beaver.

They did not find her.

But they did find Mr. Mole.

"I saw Beaver eating an ice cream cone,"

said Mr. Mole.

Everyone ran to the ice cream shop ...

... but Beaver wasn't there.

Franklin groaned.

"I give up," he said.

"I will tell my father

I lost the tin flute."

Everyone went home with Franklin.

"I have something to tell you,"

Franklin said to his father.

"I took Grandpa's tin flute.

I traded it for Rabbit's marble."

"And I traded it for Bear's pail and shovel,"

said Rabbit.

"And I traded it for Goose's sailboat,"

said Bear.

"And I traded it for Fox's crayons,"

said Goose.

"And I traded it for Skunk's kite,"

said Fox.

"And I traded it for Beaver's book,"

said Skunk.

"Hmmm,"

said Franklin's father.

"I made a trade, too."

Franklin's father reached into his pocket.

He pulled out a tin flute.

"I traded Beaver

an ice cream cone

for this tin flute,"

he said.

"*That's* Grandpa's

tin flute!"

cried Franklin.

MINITONAS EARLY YEARS SCHOOL

"Are you sure?" asked his father.

Franklin reached

for the tin flute.

Tweak! Toot! Twack!

"Oh, yes," said Franklin.

"I'm sure."